W9-BBN-911

TARTAN HOUSE

by Amanda Humann

**www.12StoryLibrary.com**



12-Story Library is an imprint of Peterson Publishing Company and Press Room Editions.

Produced for 12-Story Library by Red Line Editorial

Photographs ©: Shutterstock Images, cover, 3

Cover Design: Laura Polzin

**ISBN**
978-1-63235-160-9 (hardcover)
978-1-63235-199-9 (paperback)
978-1-62143-251-7 (hosted ebook)

**Library of Congress Control Number: 2015934304**

Printed in the United States of America
Mankato, MN
June, 2015

# CHAPTER 1

Michael's muscles burned as he shot through the water. He swam hard to keep up with the sea creatures darting ahead of him. Although they looked frightening with their jet-black eyes, ghostly-white fins, and mouths full of needle-sharp teeth, there was something strangely human about them, too. Michael wasn't afraid. Instead, he felt drawn to them, as though they shared some secret bond.

The creatures flicked their tails as if to signal to him. They skirted around a rock formation rising up from the ocean floor. Then they dropped down into a dark crevice, only to pop out of it a moment later. Michael stayed with them, swirling and dipping in the currents. He grinned as the water flowed over his skin. He felt good for once, and strong. He moved through the ocean with ease and breathed freely, even though he was underwater.

That's how he knew this was a dream. Not because he was breathing underwater, but because his lungs felt unburdened. There was no pain. His chest expanded with air, and he exhaled without coughing or hacking.

The fact that he could breathe so easily was more surprising to him than the bizarre appearance of the sea creatures swimming beside him. Yet he was puzzled by them, too. After years of being obsessed with the deep ocean, he thought he knew nearly every marine animal that had been discovered. But he had never seen anything quite like the strange, human-faced creatures in his dream.

✦ ✦ ✦ ✦ ✦

When Michael awoke, he kept his eyes closed, hoping to keep the pleasant dream running through his head like a video on repeat. But the dreamscape slowly slid away, replaced by the ping of an oxygen monitor and the hushed voices of his mother and doctor. He didn't have to listen to know what they were talking about. It was about his lungs. They were failing, and he knew it.

His mother sounded eerily calm. She spoke in the same neutral tones she had used when Michael's father had disappeared more than a year ago. His parents were research scientists who studied the ocean floor, and Michael's dad had been on a deep-ocean dive when he disappeared. Ever since, Michael's mom had refused to talk about his father or even discuss what had happened to him. She didn't show any emotion. Now she was doing it again. Was she trying to stay strong for him? Michael couldn't stand it. How could his mother be so calm? She shouldn't be calm when her son lay dying on a hospital bed.

The other voice in the room was Dr. Amir's, and it was filled with concern.

"You're still set on doing this?" he asked. "We don't know what's wrong with his lungs, so everything we do is basically an experiment. The oxygen levels we've set may not work."

"But this is his only hope," Michael's mom replied in the same reasonable tone. "Nothing else has worked. And if anything, he will have one last enjoyable experience."

Michael opened his eyes, turning toward the doctor and his mother.

"Mom? What are you talking about?"

Michael's mom quickly stepped over to his bed. Dr. Amir retreated, waving to Michael as he backed out of the room.

"You got a message from Tresh," Michael's mother said, smiling.

TreshPlaysIt! was Michael's favorite WhoToober online channel. Tresh mostly posted videos of himself playing games. But when Michael watched him, he felt as if he was really hanging out with a friend—something he hadn't been able to do for years.

"Oh, really? Did he say anything about—" Michael stopped mid-sentence, grimacing as pain shot up the sides of his neck. It felt as if jellyfish tentacles were running in lines from his shoulders to his jawline, burning tiny trails of pain as they went. He froze and clenched his eyes shut until the pain subsided. It always came in waves, and it was getting worse every day. When he could breathe, he spoke again.

"What did he say? Will he help?"

"Open it," his mom said, handing Michael his laptop.

Once his lungs had started to fail, Michael's mom said she wanted to do something special for him. She said it was to keep his mind off his illness, although he knew it was really something like a last wish.

"What would you say to taking a trip to Splashdown?" she had asked.

"Splashdown? Are you serious? Can we really go?" he had asked.

Splashdown was a one-of-a-kind hotel built on the ocean floor. His mother had told him about it when it was being designed, and he'd dreamed about visiting ever since. The hotel was situated next to a volcanic vent on the ocean floor. The area was full of underwater life. Michael imagined that looking out the windows of the hotel would be like seeing trick-or-treaters on Halloween, only instead of costumed kids, you'd see vampire squid, viperfish, and spookfish.

Although he had been dreaming about visiting Splashdown ever since he'd first heard about it, Michael was shocked that his mother was actually considering taking him there. Ever since his dad had disappeared, she hadn't gone on any more deep-water expeditions. It was as if she wanted nothing more to do with the ocean. But she told him it was for real—they were going to Splashdown. She'd been able to get a reservation at the brand-new hotel through her connections at work.

But there was one hitch. They needed to rent a deep-sea submarine to get to the hotel. And that was unbelievably expensive. Dreaming up a way to get sub money had helped Michael cope on sleepless nights, and one of those plans involved asking Tresh to help him raise the needed funds. His mom had been skeptical at first, but she'd started taking him seriously when Michael informed her that Tresh's channel had fifty million subscribers, many of whom were surprisingly generous when Tresh supported a cause. Tresh's followers had helped pay for chemotherapy for sick pets at a local animal hospital and provided funds for a talented girl with Down syndrome who wanted to make a music video. Tresh had a heart, and so did his followers.

Now, Michael hoped to be Tresh's next cause.

Michael cracked open his computer, excited about the celebrity's response. His excitement faded somewhat, though, as he read the message to his mother.

"It just says that Tresh wants to vid-chat. Should I accept? What if I say something lame when we chat and he thinks I'm lame?"

"Don't be so negative," his mother said. "He probably just wants to talk about his ideas for a fund-raiser."

"This would have been so much easier if the hotel had its own sub."

His mom sighed heavily. "The hotel was built for people with their own way to get there, like researchers and the super-rich. I guess the rest of us just have to swim."

She stuck her tongue out at him, and Michael caught a glimpse of the mother he used to know. The carefree, fun-loving mother whose husband was not missing and whose son had healthy, working lungs. That mother had started to disappear years ago, when Michael was eleven and doctors had first discovered his lungs were giving out.

The pain came back, shooting down the side of his neck. Michael squeezed his eyes shut until it went away.

# CHAPTER 2

Michael had never actually seen Tresh before. On his channel TreshPlaysIt!, viewers only saw Tresh's screen as he played his games. When their vid-chat opened, Michael almost laughed. The human Tresh was cartoonish, sporting green-tipped hair, purple jammie pants, and duck slippers.

"Hey, man!" Tresh said, leaning toward his computer's camera.

"Hey." Michael tried hard not to sound as awkward as he felt. "Hope it's okay that I e-mailed you."

"Totally cool of you to contact me," Tresh replied. "I'm down with that underwater hotel and want to help."

"Wow! Thanks, thanks so much!" Michael said.

"So," said Tresh, "I've been posting your story everywhere—Worldshouter, PlantedIt.com, PicsPoster, and now I'm about to open the official donation account on GroupMoolah. I wanted to chat live so that you knew this is for real. My subs are gonna get your sub! Get it? All I gotta do now is push Enter, and we can get you some scrilla."

"Wow, that's fast, and um . . . what?"

Tresh's face grew big on the monitor as he leaned in.

"My subscribers are gonna get you a submarine ride. I'm starting the fundraiser now to get the cash for it. That better, kid?"

"Cool. And I'm not really a kid. I'm actually sixteen."

"I'm nineteen, and I'm still a kid, but whatever works for you, bro. You ready to do this?"

Tresh's finger hovered above the Enter key on his keyboard.

"Punch it."

✦ ✦ ✦ ✦ ✦

A few hours later, a message from Tresh popped up on Michael's screen: *Pack your bags.*

"Good news," Tresh said over vid-chat. "We've raised enough for your sub—in record time, too!"

"Really?" asked Michael, elated. "That was fast! It only took, what—was it even two hours?"

"Your story just gave my subscribers the feel-goods. So many tried donating at the same time, they overwhelmed the servers at GroupMoolah. Their entire site shut down, and folks at GroupMoolah thought I was pulling a prank."

Michael couldn't believe it. His dream was coming true. If it weren't for the burning in his lungs and the pain in his neck, he would have been jumping for joy.

"So have your mom forward me the deets," Tresh said, "and I'll see you soon to give you my signature TreshPlaysIt! send-off."

# CHAPTER 3

Two weeks later, Michael found himself standing on the deck of a ship at sea. He stood near the ship's prow, looking out at the water as the ship rocked gently back and forth. It was hot outside, and the ocean's indigo surface rippled and gleamed. Michael relished breathing in the salty, ocean air.

At the stern of the ship was a squat yellow-green submersible. It was mounted on a small crane that would lower it into the water. The crew had already completed the last of the preparations for the dive, and the ship was nearly at the hotel's dive site, a couple of miles offshore.

He had been told the sub could carry only two people at a time because they also needed to haul some cargo down to the hotel. Michael would be going alone with the pilot. His mother would come down on the second dive.

As Michael looked at the submarine, he felt his mother take his hand. "This is your big day. Are you ready?"

"I've got my oxygen pack, so I'm good to go," he said. "Doc even added a silicone pad under the pack to make it more comfortable."

He shrugged his shoulders to adjust the oxygen pack that was tucked under his clothing. He had thought he'd be wearing a wet suit or something, but apparently that wasn't necessary in modern subs. Instead, he was wearing a button-down shirt and argyle sweater vest his mom had picked out. She wanted him to look nice for the pictures.

"Stop fidgeting," his mother teased as she readjusted his collar. "I wanted to get a nice picture of you before your send-off."

As he smiled for the photo, Michael spotted Tresh heading his way. Michael felt his stomach jump. He was about to meet his Internet idol.

"Here's the man, the dude, the biggest fish in the ocean—Michael!" Tresh announced.

He held up his smartphone, recording Michael.

"Uh, hi." Michael awkwardly shook Tresh's free hand. He wasn't sure what to say, and he felt self-conscious about being recorded with the bulging oxygen pack underneath his clothes.

Tresh lowered the phone.

"Relax, bro. Just say whatever you feel," Tresh said. "Your sponsors just want a glimpse of who you are. This is our thanks to them."

"I don't know," Michael said, shrugging. Suddenly, he felt like he had jellyfish swimming around in his belly. The neck pain returned full force, causing him to gasp. Tresh waited until the episode was over before he swung his phone up and prepared to start recording again.

"Okay, bud, take it easy. Just wave when I say your name," Tresh said. He turned the camera back on. "I'm here with Mikey and his mom," he began, pointing the camera at Michael and his mother, who waved and smiled.

"We're about to board the Deep Sea Vehicle Dropdeep," he intoned, in a deep voice like an announcer's. "D.S.V. Dropdeep is one of the few subs that can go all the way to the deepest parts of the ocean—more than 35,000 feet below sea level. The sub has a titanium hull for those deep-sea trips and will reach our destination in about 140 minutes."

"That's right folks, 140 minutes," Tresh continued. "That's two hours and twenty minutes—just long enough for some of you gamers to complete a campaign in Alternative Existenz! Now we know what our boy can do for fun on the ride down. I bet he can't wait to see the inside of this submarine. Let's get you on board, bro!"

Michael turned to his mother. "I'll see you in a few hours," he said. To Michael's surprise, his mother's eyes welled up with tears. She gave him a quick hug, whispering, "I love you."

As Michael headed over to the sub, he wondered where Tresh had gone. He was surprised the WhoToober didn't want to film him stepping through the sub's hatch.

The submarine looked like a huge bullet with fins. It had two portholes on each side and a bubble window in front. The hatch was on the bottom. Michael had to bend over to get into the hatch and then step up onto a short ladder. A pair of hands reached down to help pull him up.

"Hiya. I'm Al," the man helping him said. "I'm piloting your dive."

Al was a hefty man with gray hair. He pointed to the two seats near the front of the sub.

"Your seat's on the port side. Port is to your left as you face the front of the sub."

Michael nodded and then sat down. It was dark inside the sub, with only glimpses of sunlight shining in through the portholes. From what Michael could tell, the cockpit only took up a small part of the sub. There was a cargo area in back.

"You get all settled in there while I finish some paperwork," Al said. "Environmental reports need to list every bit of cargo we carry. That includes people."

Michael found his voice. "Right. They don't want the hotel dumping anything in the ocean I suppose. You know, I was reading about how they deal with garbage at Splashdown. They had to invent their own refuse system.

They send garbage to the surface in these oxygenated glass foam pods. They're covered in titanium and pressurized so that nothing can leak into the ocean. Then a boat picks them up and takes them to a sorting facility."

That was just one of the many things he'd learned about the hotel during the weeks leading up to this trip.

"Oh really? I understand leak prevention, but why oxygen?" asked Al, looking up from his clipboard.

"It kick-starts the biodegradation process. And they pressurize the trash so it isn't compacted into dense clumps from the atmospheric pressure. Apparently, oxygenated stuff biodegrades quicker at landfills," Michael explained.

"That seems like a lot of effort for trash." Al chuckled.

Al went to the back of the sub, leaving Michael to figure out the correct way to fasten the five-point harness on his seat. As he fumbled with the heavy straps, he could hear the ship's crew loading things into the cargo area.

*There must be another hatch in back,* he thought.

Al closed the hatch to the cockpit and rejoined Michael. He flipped a switch on the control panel in front. Cool air started circulating through the sub, giving Michael goose bumps.

"It gets pretty stuffy in here," Al said, taking his seat.

As Michael reached over to grab another strap, he saw movement out of the corner of his eye. He turned his head to see what it was, but it was too dark.

Then one patch of darkness stepped out of the shadows to form into a human shape. Michael blinked and looked again. The shape was still there, huddled against the cargo hatchway.

Michael reached over and tapped Al on the shoulder.

"I . . . I don't think we're alone."

# CHAPTER 4

Al turned to look at the cargo area.

"You can come out now, Mr. Tresh. I know you wanted to surprise him, but we gotta get going," said Al. "Oh, and grab the pullout seat off the wall behind Michael."

"Did that just happen? Did the surprise just get ganked by Captain Ahab? Lame! I wanted to record your reaction," said Tresh, stepping out of the dark of the cargo area and finding his seat.

"What's the big surprise?" Michael asked.

"Oh. I'm coming along for the ride!" Tresh said, lifting up his phone to record their interaction.

"What? How'd you work that out?"

"Cheddar. Kale. Cabbage."

"You made a salad?"

"No! Money, bro! We made tons—enough to cover a full ride for us all. So I decided to join you, so I can share your experience with my subscribers."

"But you said the sub can only carry two people," Michael said. While he was excited to have Tresh with him, he was a little bummed that his mother wasn't coming along as well. "That's why my mom stayed behind."

"We actually had to leave your luggage behind so your pal here could come along," Al explained. "Your mom will bring it down on the next dive."

"Oh, cool," Michael said uncertainly.

Tresh just sat and smiled, pleased with himself. He was holding up his phone and recording everything they said.

Just then, they felt the sub jerk. The crane had lifted it up and was moving it out over the water. Next, there was a sudden drop as the sub was lowered into the water. Soon, they were bobbing up and down in the ocean.

While Al was busy talking on the radio, Michael leaned toward Tresh.

"Does my mom know you're on board?"

"Nope, I don't think so," Tresh said, shaking his head. "I paid for three, and the sub company didn't care what order we went in. She probably thinks it's just you and Pilot Party Pooper in here. I ninja'd my way into the cargo hatch so I could surprise you. I'm gonna rocket to the top of the likes list with this vid." Tresh shook his phone.

"What about the hotel? Are you staying there, too?"

"I wish! I'm just going to record your arrival and get some shots of Splashdown itself. Then I'll come back up. I couldn't get reservations. The hotel doesn't have a website, and I can't find contact info for it anywhere. How'd your mom do it?"

Michael shrugged, clicking the last part of his harness in place.

"She said they don't have a website because they only do business with a small group of people, so there's no need to advertise. She works for an ocean seismology research group, and she got me in through them."

"Seismo-wha?"

"She's an earthquake scientist, who focuses on the ocean floor. She and my dad both worked for the ocean research group, but he worked on underwater structures as an engineer."

"Why didn't he come today?"

"He . . . uh . . . disappeared about a year ago," Michael said, fiddling with the ends of the straps on his harness.

"Oh. How?"

"Well, he was on an expedition, and something happened. I don't know what exactly," Michael said. For the thousandth time, he felt angry with his mother for not telling him more about his dad's disappearance. Maybe she thought she was protecting him, but he deserved to know. People always wanted to know what happened, and he never really knew what to say.

"He was working. He'd usually go out on a research ship for a few days, or even a week, but be back by the weekend," he explained. "Saturday mornings he'd teach me computer coding, which I secretly hated, but I did it anyway just to spend that little extra time with him."

Michael wasn't sure why he was adding such personal information to the story, especially with Tresh recording everything he said. But secretly, he hoped that maybe one of the WhoToober subscribers might see it and possibly have information about his dad. So anything he said might help.

"Anyway, one of the marine biologists on board saw him on her way into their morning meeting. She said he was staring down at some flying fish jumping near the boat. When the meeting started and he wasn't there, she went to get him. He was nowhere to be found. Nobody knows what happened, and my mom refuses to talk about it."

"Whoa . . . sorry." Tresh grimaced and raised his eyebrows. "I can't believe you're willing to get on this sub after that, bro."

"It's okay. He taught me everything about the deep ocean, so down there, I'll feel like I'm close to him again."

Al turned to them.

"All right, boys, we're ready to dive."

Michael watched the water first cover the windows, and then gradually darken as they descended. He knew that once they left the surface, they'd have about 650 feet in the sunlight zone before light would virtually disappear. He looked eagerly for silvery schools of tuna or a sleek shark, but all he saw were lots of jellyfish. Within minutes, the sub dropped into the darker water. He switched to looking for swordfish, since they'd been found as deep as 1,970 feet, but it was hard to see, and soon, all he could see was whatever came into view in front of the sub's lights. He was disappointed that Tresh quickly lost interest and spent the bulk of the trip focused on his smartphone.

Eventually, Tresh left whatever off-line game he was playing and returned to reality. He looked out the front window.

"Look out there. Nothing but black water. It's kind of freaky," said Tresh. "No mermaid hotties, no enemy subs to shoot. Remind me why you wanted to come here again?"

Michael turned to stare at him.

"Seriously? This is ninety-five percent of earth's living space, and it's barely been explored. Don't you wonder what's down here?"

"Nope. I'm a feet-on-ground, head-in-the-Internet kind of guy."

"But this is totally cool. It's like outer space—it's dark, it's alien, and everyone wonders what kind of life is out there. But here every little point of light *is* life. Any light you see is usually made by some kind of ocean life, like hatchetfish, squid, or dragonfish."

"Okay, that makes it sound way cooler. You're talking about that biolumie—luma—bio—"

"Bioluminescence?"

"Yeah." Tresh inhaled sharply, and then yelled, "What the heck is that?"

"It's lights created by living things. I have lung issues, not ear issues—you don't need to yell."

"No, *that!*" Tresh yelled again, scrambling farther back in his seat and pointing to the cockpit window. An enormous reddish-brown blob about three feet wide floated under the lights.

"It's a jellyfish," laughed Al. "A right big one, but still just a jellyfish."

Michael shook his head and looked out his own window, while Tresh complained he couldn't get good pictures with his phone.

Although he was excited to get to Splashdown, the long ride was making Michael sleepy. As his eyelids started to droop, he caught a glimpse of something in the water outside the porthole nearest him. In the light from the sub, the object glowed a bright white. It was either very tiny or very far away—he couldn't tell which—and it looked like a slender, pale fish. Gradually the fish seemed to grow larger in his view, and Michael realized it was swimming toward the sub. As the fish drew near, Michael saw its long pectoral fins and huge dark eyes.

Michael broke out into a cold sweat as the thing turned, its fins extending.

He recognized the creature from his dreams.

# CHAPTER 5

As quickly as it had appeared, the strange fish vanished into the black ocean water. Michael spent the rest of the trip looking out every window, trying to catch another glimpse of the creature and trying to convince Al and Tresh to do the same. When they finally got to the hotel, Michael was still searching the ocean.

"Michael, forget about the fish person already," said Tresh. "It's time to go in."

"I know what I saw!" Michael insisted, irritated. He looked out the porthole window again and squinted. They had arrived at the hotel, but it was impossible to see any of the structure except the lights that marked the airlock on the outside. Al opened the hatch into the airlock room.

"Ready?" Al asked, turning to Michael.

Michael nodded, and then climbed out of the sub and followed Tresh into the small airlock room.

"Okay," Al called out from inside the sub. "The hotel confirmed that after I seal the outer door, the inner door will unlock, and you can go inside, where the staff will meet you. Michael, I'll be back in a few hours with your mom."

They said their good-byes, and after the outer door was sealed, Tresh turned to Michael.

"Back to the fish thing. I didn't see it, Al didn't see it, and you said it looked just like a thing from a dream you always have. You were in la-la land and dreamed it. Now that we're actually at Splashdown, you can't get all cray-cray mermaid fish freak in front of anyone, okay?" Tresh patted Michael on the arm as if he were a small, confused child. "This is your real dream, remember? Right here. The hotel. *This* is happening."

"Okay, okay," Michael said, feeling his cheeks heating up. He knew what he had seen was no dream, but it was no use arguing. He reached for the door handle to enter the hotel lobby. Tresh put out a hand and stopped him.

"Whoa, whoa, whoa. Wait a sec," Tresh said. "Check yourself. You can't be so basic or the Internet will tear you up. I know you have this lung thing going on, but you gotta make an entrance."

"I've spent most of the last few years in a hospital bed because of this 'lung thing,' as you put it," Michael said. "I haven't really practiced making entrances."

He was already humiliated that Al and Tresh refused to believe what he had seen outside the window. And now Tresh's advice was just making him feel even more clumsy and awkward.

"Don't worry, bro, I got your back," said Tresh, pulling out his phone, swiping and tapping at it. "Can't tell you all my secrets, but I do have some tricks up my sleeves to make you look great."

Michael let out a deep sigh. He knew he should feel grateful to Tresh, but he was starting to get a little annoyed about the big production Tresh made out of everything. Michael just wanted to get inside the hotel. This is what he had been waiting for for weeks.

"Let's see . . . triumphant theme music!" Tresh said into his phone, and an upbeat song began to play.

"Now, let's lose the sweater vest," he continued, tugging at Michael's argyle vest in disdain. "And unbutton a button or two on your shirt. You need to look like a teenager, not an accountant."

"Okay, okay, you don't have to strip me," Michael said, brushing Tresh's hands aside. He took off the vest and fixed his shirt. He worried that the oxygen pack under his shirt would be more obvious without the sweater vest.

Tresh stood back and eyeballed him. "Still not quite there. Huh. Oh—I got it!" He reached over and ruffled Michael's hair. Then he grabbed Michael by the elbow and spun him around to face the door into the hotel.

"Nailed it. You look so awesome I gotta high five myself. Okay, bro, you ready?"

Tresh didn't wait for him to respond. He lifted the phone and began recording.

"Ta-da!" Tresh yanked the door open and thrust Michael into the blinding lights of the hotel lobby.

# CHAPTER 6

Michael squinted under the bright lights angled to shine at the door. He and Tresh stood alone in a very small, deserted hallway that opened up into a larger room. It was dim beyond the lights, so he couldn't really see much.

"This doesn't look much like a lobby," whispered Michael. "It's more like an entryway into someone's house."

He hadn't been in many hotels, but the few he'd seen had warm, bright, welcoming entryways and lobbies.

"It's a good thing I came along with you," said Tresh, shielding his eyes against the lights, "or you'd be super-single. Where's the welcome wagon? There isn't even a check-in desk, or signs to tell us where to go. Fail. Hello? Hell-o-o!"

"Wow, this place is really different," said Michael, blinking and trying to get a better view of the room that spread out from the entryway.

"Maybe they got your arrival time wrong, and the staff are having lunch or something. Speaking of which, you know, I could use some chow."

Michael's eyes adjusted as he peered into the dimly-lit room, and details started to appear. "It's like a big underwater-themed living room," he said.

Tresh walked up alongside Michael. The walls were all light blue-green, and they shimmered as if made from crushed diamonds lit from behind the wall. And there wasn't a sharp edge anywhere—everything was rounded off. Michael touched the wall, and it felt like hardened sand.

"This isn't what I expected at all," said Michael. "I thought the walls and floors would be some sort of new plastic or concrete, and it would look more . . . more high tech."

The floor was covered in the same hard material as the walls, but it was gray in color and not shimmery. The few pieces of furniture were see-through and inflatable with rubber handles on the sides like rafts. They faced a huge window that ran from the ceiling almost to the floor.

"Weird. Why would they have a huge window when you can't see anything?" asked Tresh.

Michael stared out at the darkness, but saw only a reflection of himself. A flutter of pain started in his neck but subsided.

"Ask the staff when we find them," Michael replied. "*If* we find them."

"Stand down, Captain Pessimistic," said Tresh. "They're here. Al said he talked to someone before departing."

There were two hallways leading off the lobby. Michael and Tresh split up. Michael took the right hallway and found a kitchen and an empty dining area. The walls of the hallway had a pattern of small holes, each as wide as his pinkie. Michael thought it was a cool way to disguise drain holes. At the end of the hall there was a smooth ramp that led up to a platform made from a metal grate. On one side was an open area for waste disposal, where trash pods half as tall as Michael sat in huge clear tubes ready for launch. Across the platform on the other side was a control room. No one was here, either. Michael decided to keep looking around.

One half of the control room was filled with pipes and several gauges. On the opposite side of the room there were multiple monitors all connected to one ancient computer workstation. It wasn't the tech Michael expected. Curious, Michael read what was on each monitor.

When he got to one labeled "life support," he noticed a chart that showed a line slanting downward from left to right. It was labeled "Oxygen." He felt a twinge in his neck again.

"That can't be right," he said out loud, following the slope of the line with his finger, and double-checking all the labels on the chart.

Tresh came running into the room, panting. "Oh, thank God I found you. All I saw were a few empty bedrooms and a bathroom. One. What kind of a hotel has one bathroom?"

He inhaled and then coughed. "And there are no signs of people anywhere."

"None?"

"I opened every door and looked into every cubbyhole," Tresh said. "There's nobody here. Not a soul."

Tresh's panic actually had the opposite effect on Michael. He felt himself consciously growing calmer and more focused. This was something he had trained himself to do because of his lung condition. Freaking out about things would only cause him to have breathing difficulties. So, although on the inside he was just as worried as Tresh, Michael remained calm.

"Let me check something," he said, going back to the workstation. He tapped the keyboard a few times and was surprised there wasn't any security software to get through before he began clicking through menus on the main screen.

"Okay, but where is everyone?" continued Tresh. "We can't possibly be alone. Who did Al talk to? This isn't right. I mean, I am surrounded by people all day, every day. Even though they aren't there physically, they're still there. I haven't gone this long without one ping, like . . . ever. I can feel my heart racing. I think I'm about to lose it, bro."

"We have a much worse problem than being alone," Michael said suddenly, looking up from the monitor.

"Whaaa?"

"This computer is monitoring the oxygen levels in here. According to this readout, the oxygen levels in the life support systems are dropping, and they'll continue dropping," said Michael. "But that's not the worst part."

Tresh grabbed his throat and waited for Michael to continue.

"It was done on purpose."

# CHAPTER 7

"So, we're going to suffocate to death? Are you for real?" Tresh screeched, beginning to hyperventilate.

"For real. And try not to panic. You'll only use up the oxygen we have left that much more quickly," Michael said. He already knew how to regulate his own breathing, but he knew he'd need more oxygen soon. His oxygen pack was getting low. He had more of them, but they were with his luggage, which had been left behind because of Tresh.

"H-how do you know it was done on purpose?"

"The system appears to be functioning normally, and the log shows an entry right here that it was manually programmed to change oxygen levels. But why would anybody do that?"

"How should I know? It's like some sick joke! How long do we have?"

Michael almost laughed out loud at Tresh's reaction. While he was also worried about what was happening, death was an everyday concern for Michael. He was never really sure from day to day whether his lungs would give out on him. So while Tresh was freaking out, Michael's thoughts were spinning, trying to figure out what was going on.

"I'm not really sure. It looks like it reduces over a few days, but it drops to seventy-five percent of normal in just a few hours. I don't know how long two people can live on that."

"Change it back!"

"I can't. There's no on or off check-box."

"We've got to get help! Let's call Al!"

Michael looked away, feeling like he'd let Tresh down. And he was about to do it again.

"Tresh, did you find any other control rooms, or maybe things that looked like the radio on the sub?"

"Nope."

"Then I can't contact Al."

"Why not?"

"Because there's no communication system here. None. At. All."

Tresh was silent for once. The only sound he made was a tiny wheeze as he tried to inhale lightly.

"The controls are set up for a communication system. See this place on this monitor that says 'CMU'? See how it's blank? There's nothing there. Maybe it was never installed. Or, judging by the oxygen issue . . . maybe it's been removed."

"The sub!" said Tresh, "That's it! Al will be back in a few hours and then we can go back. Crisis over."

"I just hope it can carry all of us at one time," Michael said.

There was silence again.

"I don't feel so good," said Tresh.

"Oh . . . wow," Michael said, looking at Tresh. "You are turning totally gray. Maybe you should lie down." He looked around the control room, but there wasn't a soft surface. "Let's get you out to the lobby." He put Tresh's arm over his shoulders and led him slowly back out to the couches. He picked the biggest one in front of the window and helped Tresh lie down. Then, Michael sat down next to his friend. After years of having people taking care of him, it felt strange to Michael to be taking care of someone else.

They both stared at the blackness outside the window.

✦ ✦ ✦ ✦ ✦

Michael eventually felt his confidence return. He'd been feeling awkward and self-conscious around Tresh, who was older and more savvy. But now, with Tresh curled up in a ball on the sofa, Michael felt he was the stronger and more knowledgeable of the two. To Tresh, the idea of death was new and terrifying. But Michael had been thinking about death and dying for years now. That didn't mean he wasn't scared. It just meant he knew how not to let the fear of death overcome him. If he hadn't figured out how to do that, he would have had to spend every minute of every hour of the past few years curled up in a ball just like Tresh was right now.

"You okay, Tresh?" he asked.

"I just need a moment, bro."

Michael didn't know what else to do other than distract Tresh and himself.

"There must be a reason for this window. There's gotta be outside lights or something," he said, standing up to touch the glass.

Slowly, he began walking around the living room, running his hands over the wall. The scratchy texture felt familiar and comfortable under his fingers. He stopped when he felt a slight crack in the finish next to the window. As he prodded at it, a panel slid open to reveal several buttons.

He pushed the button labeled "main." The lights in the room dimmed. At the same time, a light came on outside the window.

"Hey, Tresh, take a look at this," he said, hoping to distract Tresh by pretending to be fascinated by the view outside. "You know how the two halls stick out at open angles from the lobby living room? It makes a courtyard outside the window. I can see where some of the pipes from the control room go out in the water under the building." As more outside lights came on in sequence from the lobby out to the ends of the wings, Tresh got up and joined Michael at the window. Soon, Michael saw that he did not have to pretend to be fascinated by the view. The oceanscape outside looked like a scene from another planet.

"Whoa, what is that?" Tresh rasped as the last lights at the end of the courtyard finally came on, casting light into the darkness.

In the distance, framed in the center of the window, loomed what looked like a miniature undersea volcano, spewing clouds high into the water. Lumpy spires of rock jutted up around it.

"That's a black smoker. It's basically an undersea geyser," said Michael. "And those fields of what look kind of like skinny red tulips growing out of long white tubes? Those are giant tubeworms. They look small from here, but really they're huge. Some even grow over six feet long."

"Look at the side of the geyser. There's like a bubbly white crust on it, and it's moving. It's gonna blow, bro!" said Tresh, backing away from the window.

"Relax. All that white stuff is a huge mass of crabs hanging out together. And I see some giant mussels, too! I didn't expect to see those," Michael said, excitedly. "I can't believe all those creatures can survive that extreme heat. It's cold in the ocean, but some of those vents can produce—wait, am I boring you?"

Michael found it strange, but talking about the ocean life took his mind off their current situation. It was almost like he was now the WhoToober and Tresh was one of his subscribers.

"Nope. If I'm gonna die, at least I have a cool view," Tresh laughed. "Hey, did you turn the lights off?"

The lights on the right wing flickered and faded, and as they did, shadows encroached on the view. One shadow moved. Another shadow moved, and then two more.

"Wasn't me." As Michael said it, a dull thud sent vibrations through the floor of the hotel. Another thud came, and then another. Clouds of sediment billowed out from under the right wing and swirled slowly in the water of the courtyard.

"Giant tubeworms, giant mussels." Tresh retreated to the couch, panting. "What else is giant down here, Michael?"

"Giant squid."

# CHAPTER 8

"But if you're thinking that was a giant squid, Tresh, think again. They are big, but they wouldn't attack a building. Giant squid eat things in the water—mostly things smaller than people."

Michael stared out the window, not sure what he expected to see. The shadows weren't moving and the sediment had settled, but the lights on the right wing were flickering on and off.

Michael closed his eyes, feeling a little tightness in his neck. "Tresh?" he asked.

"Yeah?"

"Check out that pipe out there. Does it look like it's broken or something?"

"Yeah, it does. It looks like there's a big gaping hole in it. Like something bit it. Why? Is that bad?"

"That depends on what the pipe is for. There's something stenciled on the pipe. Can you read it?"

Tresh came back to the window, slowly, like he was afraid some giant sea monster would burst through the glass and swallow him whole. He peered out at the pipe under the flickering lights.

"It starts with a 'W' . . . I think there's an 'A' . . ."

Tresh put his nose to the window and squinted.

"Water inlet. The hole is on the water inlet pipe."

"A hole in the water inlet pipe means we may not have to worry about oxygen," said Michael, sighing.

"That's good!" said Tresh.

"Not really. We may drown before we run out of air."

# CHAPTER 9

"You really are a downer, you know that? I can't even . . . I just can't." Tresh flopped back on the couch.

"I'll go check the control room—you stay here," said Michael.

"No prob. I'm just gonna record my last words."

In the control room, everything looked to be in order. The monitor for the plumbing system showed that everything was functioning normally.

"There must be a valve between the leak and the house. Hope it holds. One problem down, now back to figuring out the oxygen." He realized he was talking to himself, so he yelled it again down the hall, and heard a faint affirmative answer from Tresh.

Michael didn't realize he was holding his breath until he let it out. As it whispered past his lips, he checked his oxygen, and realized it was empty. He wondered how long it had been that way and how long it would be before Al returned with his luggage and the extra oxygen packs. It'd be too late, he knew.

Michael pulled the useless oxygen off his back, stretched his arms, and inhaled, feeling strangely good. He'd helped Tresh to the lobby living room, and he'd walked all around the room searching for light switches. Normally, even that small amount of activity would have totally exhausted him. But just now, he didn't feel exhausted at all. Maybe facing certain death was giving him some sort of adrenalin boost. It probably wouldn't be long before he was weak and useless again, he thought, so he'd better try to save them while he could.

Michael went back to the computer. If someone could make the oxygen level drop, maybe he could stop it somehow. All he had to do was find the lines of code that had changed the system and undo them. He scanned the list of entries, looking for any changes that matched the time on the log. There were way more entries than he'd expected, but halfway down the list, he finally found the line that made the change in the oxygen level.

After fourteen tries, Michael thought he had finally succeeded in rewriting the line of code to stop the oxygen from dropping. He crossed his fingers and pressed the Enter key.

When the monitor showed the oxygen staying at a steady level, he let out a sigh of relief. The oxygen wasn't back to the level where it had started, but he had stopped any further decrease. He silently thanked his Dad for having taught him what he knew about coding.

As he pushed away from the computer workstation to go share the good news, he heard a slightly muffled scream from the living room.

# CHAPTER 10

Before he could stop to think that he shouldn't be running, Michael ran toward the living room.

Tresh was curled up on the couch, staring out the window.

"What's wrong?"

"Them! Those things. I see the fish people, Michael."

"You saw them? More than one? Out there?" Michael jerked a thumb at the window.

"Yes. I mean no. There's no way they are real, so the lack of oxygen must be getting to me. That's gotta be it. I'm hallucinating! But why are my hallucinations the same as your dream?"

Michael searched the view out the window. "There's nothing out there now. A lot of stuff happens when you have low blood oxygen levels: weakness, slurred speech, dizziness. You're probably right. You probably were hallucinating. Good news is I stopped the oxygen level from decreasing! I couldn't figure out how to get it back to where they started, but things won't get any worse."

Michael plopped onto the couch. Now that one crisis had been averted, he felt exhausted.

Tresh inhaled deeply and grinned. "Thank goodness it won't get any worse. Missing staff, no oxygen, possible drowning, freaky fish people . . ."

"I get it," said Michael. "But I have to admit, some part of me was hoping the fish people were real."

Tresh stopped grinning and stared out the window again. When Michael turned to look, his heart thudded in his chest and his neck fluttered with the beginnings of that familiar jellyfish sting of pain.

Three huge fish people floated outside the window, looking in. They were the size of humans and had human-like heads with huge solid black eyes, just like the creatures from Michael's dreams but more familiar somehow. Their necks and shoulders led to human arms that ended in webbed hands with claws. From the chest down, their bodies were covered in pinkish-white scales, and instead of legs they had muscled fish tails. They floated vertically like seahorses.

"Are you sure you got the air fixed, bro? 'Cause I'm seeing things again. And I know it's a hallucination, because one looks a lot like your . . ."

Michael stopped him and went to the window to put his hand on it.

"Mom, Dr. Amir? And . . . Dad?"

# CHAPTER 11

The creature that looked like his mother swam closer and put her webbed hand against his on the other side of the glass. She looked right at him.

"Michael!"

Michael realized he must have been hearing his mom call his name in his head. Her mouth didn't even move. It was definitely his mother's voice, although it was filled with more emotion than he was used to hearing from the calm, rational mother he'd left above water.

He felt a twinge in his neck. Maybe the increase in oxygen was giving him some weird sort of head rush, and he was imagining everything—hallucinating, just like Tresh.

"Michael, look at me! Don't be afraid!" the voice came again.

"Geez, bro, look at her already, so she'll stop shouting! Man, she's loud," said Tresh, grabbing his forehead. "And I can't plug my ears, 'cause she's talking in my head!"

"You can hear her, too?"

"Of course he can," Mom-fish said. "I'm one of the best at communicating telepathically with humans because I'm half human."

"Are the others really Dr. Amir and . . . Dad?" Michael asked, pointing to the other two creatures outside the window.

The Dad thing swam over and nodded.

"We sure are. You look great, kiddo. I can tell being down here has already had an effect."

"And you look . . . weird, Dad. Is this for real? I can hear you in my head, too. Are you, um, half human, like . . . Mom?"

"Yes."

Michael inhaled. This had to be a dream. Maybe he'd wake up in his hospital bed in a second. And, yet, it seemed real, too. And if his parents were fish creatures . . .

"What does that make me?" Michael asked.

Dr. Amir exchanged looks with Mom and Dad. They nodded.

"We are the Finn," Dr. Amir said. His voice was deeper and harder to hear. "Your parents are each half Finn, but you are the first child to be born to two halflings. We cannot tell which genes you have inherited from each parent. So we don't know what you are—not yet.

"Full Finn have control over changing back and forth from human to Finn when they are a year old. Yet, you have stayed in human form, so we assumed—" The doctor turned and looked off in the distance. "I feel something nearby. I'll go check the perimeter."

Michael looked back at Tresh. He was straining to hear, his brow furrowed.

"I got nothin'," Tresh said, shrugging. "Couldn't understand a thing that one said. Too bad, thish ish pretty much the coolesht thing I've ever experienshed," he said, slurring his words a little.

*Tresh must be getting tired from the lack of oxygen,* Michael thought.

"He talks," said Michael, "just probably too low for you to hear him. I guess he must be a full Finn."

"Full what?" Tresh croaked.

"Honey," said Mom, grabbing his attention again, "when you started having lung issues a few years back, we thought that you were just a really late bloomer. This last year, you started showing signs that you were about to convert into your Finn form for the first time, but your transformation wasn't following any predictable pattern, and the change was taking so long, we didn't really know what to do."

Up until now, Michael had felt pretty numb to the idea of death. The fear of dying had been such a part of his daily life that he grew numb to it. Yet now, now that he was learning that he wasn't actually dying, but just different, the numbness was quickly fading and being replaced with an incredible joy. He smiled out the window at his parents.

"That's why I spent most of the last year building this place," his dad said. "I did it so you could get used to the deep ocean before making the transition to come out here."

"Wait, we *own* Splashdown? No wonder it looked more like a house than a hotel! Do you mean we can actually live here?"

Michael's heart beat so hard he was sure it could be felt on the inflatable couch behind him.

"I missed you, kiddo," said Dad. "I could communicate with Mom and Doc from here, but we thought it might not be a good idea for my voice to just pop into your head. And with your condition getting worse, I needed to focus on finishing this house. I couldn't exactly hire a construction crew down here, so I worked nonstop, doing it myself."

"That must have been a ton of work," Michael said, glancing around at the house.

"Although we have some powers that humans don't, it was still a lot of work for one person to do. And I have to admit I didn't plan everything as well as I could have. I used the best computer we could afford, and until I had to communicate with Al, I didn't think about the fact that we might need a communications system."

"So it was you who talked to Al," said Tresh.

"Yep, he used his sub's communication system and I replied telepathically."

The doctor came back to the window.

"We have a complication or two in our experiment. I see you took your oxygen off, and that's good, because you have to reduce your oxygen at the right rate or you won't make the transition into Finn form, and you'll die. We set an oxygen reduction program in the house to take care of you and make the transition easier. I just didn't realize you'd have a full human with you."

Michael's throat shut tight, which was a good thing, since he did not want to say out loud what everyone was thinking: that Tresh needed oxygen and Michael needed to avoid oxygen. One of them was going to die.

# CHAPTER 12

"Why's everyone look so serious all of a sudden?" asked Tresh, his eyes blinking slowly. "Why don't I feel better?"

"Tresh, you look awful."

"Thanks a lot, bro."

Michael explained their situation to Tresh as best he could, and then turned back to the window.

"Why isn't he getting better? I stopped the oxygen reduction program."

"You what?" Mom covered her mouth with her pale-clawed hands. "Why would you do that?"

"I thought we were going to die if I didn't! But I only stopped it from decreasing further. I couldn't get it back up to normal."

"Relax," said Dr. Amir, putting his hand on Mom's shoulder. "We don't really know what oxygen levels Michael needs at this point. We just know they have to go down, and that they can't increase or he might die.

"Bring Tresh over here by the window so I can get a look at him," Dr. Amir communicated, pointing to the corner of the window with better lighting.

Michael helped him up, and the doctor looked Tresh over and asked him questions. Michael's father translated for him, since Tresh couldn't hear the doctor. While the doctor looked at Tresh, Michael talked to his mother.

"Why didn't you tell me what I am, Mom? That I was going to go through this change and that I'm a Finn?"

"When you were little, we thought you were completely human. But as you grew, you started changing. Originally, I was going to tell you once we got to the hotel and ease you into the idea, but . . . well, here we are."

Dr. Amir was done with his inspection. Tresh fell onto the couch and lay there with his eyes closed.

"Tresh is suffering from the effects of low oxygen levels in his blood," said the doctor. "He'll get better, but only if we can get him to a human hospital where he can be properly treated."

Michael thought for a moment. "He can go back on the sub when the pilot comes back with it. Wait, Mom, you're already here, so is Al even coming back?"

"No. I told him I had an emergency and needed to get back to shore, so we postponed the second trip. Dr. Amir met me at the docks. We got to Splashdown just before you guys arrived."

"How is that possible?"

"In groups, we have . . . abilities," said Dr. Amir, looking sideways at Tresh's limp form. Michael took the hint and dropped the subject.

"So you were here when the lights went off and on and there was all that noise on the right wing?"

"Yep, that was us," said Dad. "We saw Tresh on the sub as you came down, so we stayed out here and tried to figure out what to do. There's a big squid that hunts here, and she showed up after your sub arrived. When you turned the courtyard lights on, it was like turning on a fast-food sign. We were trying to turn them off from outside when she attacked. She ruined the airlock controls both inside and out when she hit the side of the house. Now we can't come inside. We decided to let Tresh see us so we could figure out how to get him out."

"What about the squid?" asked Michael.

"That was another of the complications that I mentioned," said the doctor. "She hasn't left the area, and in fact—"

The building shuddered as a huge tentacle swept down from above and smacked into the glass.

# CHAPTER 13

Tresh's eyes must have been open when the squid attacked, because he let out a pathetic dry scream that croaked out until he sat still, panting.

For two seconds, Michael saw a flash of suckers and multiple huge catlike claws as the fleshy end of the tentacle grabbed at the window. Then the tentacle ripped away as Dr. Amir and his parents fled with the squid in hot pursuit.

"Mom! Dad! Doc?" Michael yelled, but they were gone. Clouds of stirred-up sediment filled the courtyard, obscuring his view.

"See? Giant squid. Just like I thought. I was right!" Tresh said, gasping. Then he collapsed flat on the couch, one arm dropping to the floor.

"That actually was a colossal squid."

"I said giant, isn't that big enough for you?"

"Colossal's not just another way to describe the squid. That's its name!" said Michael, looking into the courtyard for the squid and his family.

"Colossal squid. That's a thing?"

"It's a thing. A very scary thing. Colossal squid have larger, heavier bodies than giant squid, and they have the largest known eyes in the entire animal kingdom. Where giant squid have eyes on each side of their head, colossal squid eyes face forward like a land predator's eyes. And those eyes have organs in them that create bioluminescence. Basically they have their own headlights. And with all this added light, it's like they can see in high definition."

"And?"

"Remember how I said giant squid eat mostly small prey? Colossal squid feed on deep-water toothfish that grow to six and a half feet."

"Man-sized."

"Yep, same size as something else, too."

"Your fam."

"Yep, the Finn. That squid has great eyesight, and when it can't see, it can use its headlights. You can't hide from it. And how do you fight it? On each of those two long tentacles, it has multiple claws that can swivel 360 degrees to grab anything. My family is being hunted by the perfect deep-ocean predator." Michael could feel pressure building in his neck, and a rushing sound filled his ears.

Tresh looked down at the floor where his hand was resting. He held it up, limp and dripping wet. "Why is there water on the floor?" he slurred.

# CHAPTER 14

Michael crouched down next to Tresh. A puddle was growing on the floor. When he sniffed, he confirmed his fear: it was salt water.

"Where is this coming from?" Michael asked.

Tresh just shrugged, his breathing ragged as he watched Michael look for the source of the puddle.

Michael glanced at the window, thinking maybe the force of the tentacle slamming against it had broken the waterproofing seals around the glass. The wall was dry.

Outside, the sediment in the courtyard had mostly settled, but there was still a low layer of it above the ocean floor.

By the pipes under the right wing, the sediment was flowing up instead of down, as though being swept up in a current. Michael grew cold when he saw where the water was going—it was rushing straight into the hole in the water inlet pipe, as if being sucked by a vacuum. He looked to the right wing and saw that the rushing sound was coming from water spurting out of the holes in the walls.

"Tresh, water is coming in the hole in the water inlet pipe. A valve must have broken!"

Tresh lay motionless on the couch, his arm hanging limp and his hand near the floor. The water swirled around his hand like a creek running around a rock.

"Tresh? Tresh!" Michael yelled, kneeling by the couch and shaking his friend so hard that Tresh's green hair wagged back and forth. He saw Tresh's chest rising and falling. He was still breathing, just unconscious.

Now it was all up to Michael. Unsure of what to do, he turned to the window, wishing his parents would return to help him, but it was still quiet and there was no sign of them, or of the doctor.

"What do I do?" he asked the ocean. It did not respond.

His neck tightened in pain. Michael reached for the floor to steady himself, but only succeeded in dunking his forearms in the puddle that was now a few inches deep.

Tendrils of tension crept down his neck, and his skin felt like it was ripping. He breathed through the pain, staying still on his hands and knees in the water. He was hot from the effort of not collapsing, so the water didn't feel as icy-cold as he thought it would be. It felt really good. He wanted to duck into it, but it wasn't deep enough, and he still wasn't sure he should immerse himself yet, not knowing what stage of transformation his body was at.

He lifted his head, splashed his face, and got up to see if he could figure out a way to stop the water in the control room.

Running through the hall was torture, as water shot out of the holes at pressure so high he thought it would cut his skin. He tried to run up the center of the hallway where the streams had less force, and he managed to make it up the ramp and into the control room.

Frantic, Michael checked the monitor for plumbing again, but this time, he clicked through until he saw a map of the pipes. He traced the pipes across the screen and saw two valves on the water inlet pipe. They were the only valves between the end of the pipe and the control room, and they were under the house, so he couldn't get to them. He gulped, hoping he could use the computer to fix whatever was wrong.

He checked the status of the valves, expecting to see a malfunction. All the monitor said was "normal and functioning." It didn't make any sense.

There was nothing he could do.

Michael turned and walked out onto the platform. His legs dragged, and he stumbled as he tried to cross the room. Another spasm of pain seized the sides of his neck, and he sank to the floor.

He was weak and useless again.

# CHAPTER 15

Michael wanted to be out in the living room with Tresh, waiting for his family to return. But he knew that if there was any way to save Tresh from drowning, the answer would be somewhere here in the control room. He crawled to the door, wrapped his hands around the back of his neck and leaned back against the doorjamb.

A powerful cough rattled from his shaky body.

For years, death had been a familiar part of Michael's vocabulary. He thought he'd made peace with the fact that it was probably coming sooner rather than later. But now he realized he was not nearly ready to die after all. Especially now that he knew his dreams were real, and literally within reach.

He needed more time.

He needed more energy.

He needed less oxygen in the air—but Tresh needed more.

Michael thought about Tresh. Tresh was a good guy. He'd said yes when Michael needed help. He'd helped so many others, too. There was no way Michael could abandon him.

The world needed people like Tresh.

Michael eased up off of the floor and slowly, carefully walked to the computer station. He took a deep breath, opened up the oxygen program again, and started trying new lines of code.

Michael tried several different ways to increase the oxygen level. Each time he felt like he was getting close, but the code wouldn't work. He reversed the terms in the original commands and tried inventing whole new ways to approach the system. Beads of sweat formed on his upper lip.

The letters and numbers on the screen seemed to run into each other. He stopped and rubbed his eyes and ears. Then, he got up and half-walked, half-stumbled to the doorway. He looked out and down the hall, and his heart jumped.

The water level had reached at least two feet up the walls. There was so much water flowing in that it was making its own current.

Michael lurched to the edge of the platform and dropped into the river in the hallway, thinking only of Tresh unconscious on the couch in the living room. Images of him falling off the couch and silently drowning filled Michael's mind.

Michael waded through the middle of the hallway with grim determination, moving as quickly as he could to get out of the slicing saltwater streams. The incoming water created a current flowing into the living room, so he did not have much resistance since it was going his way.

When he reached the living room, he was relieved to see Tresh still safely on the couch—

and the couch floating. The only part of Tresh that was covered by water was his hand, trailing as the couch bumped into the lower part of the window.

The window was still empty—no parents, no doctor, no squid. Michael wasn't sure how he felt about that. He couldn't help them and they couldn't help him right now, anyway. But he never thought he'd be alone when he died.

He checked Tresh and was glad to see he was still breathing.

"Tresh, I know you can't hear me, but I'm going to talk to you because I know neither of us wants to die alone.

"I thought I could save you, and I really, really tried. The flooding just increased big-time, and I don't know how to fix that. Even if I seal off the right wing to stop more water from coming into this section, you'd still die, because I can't get the oxygen program's code right.

"Now I'm not sure I can save either of us. I'm useless. That squid totally trashed this place, Tresh. We're never getting out of here."

Trash. Tresh.

As soon as the words came out of his mouth, Michael found that he had one last idea.

As the idea grew, he thought maybe it wouldn't work, but he didn't have time to even consider that it would fail. There was nothing to lose.

The water now flowed around Tresh's hand rapidly, like waves being cut by the bow of a boat. That felt wrong, as Tresh was the only dry thing in the entire house. Michael reached over and lifted Tresh's hand from the water and placed it across his chest.

"Gotta get you over to the platform at the end of the right wing. It's not that much higher than the middle section of the house, but it's high enough to keep you out of the water longer. You get to go for a ride, my friend."

He grabbed the rubber handle at the end of the couch and started pulling it to the right wing, leading with his back.

The current was stronger now that he was going against it, and it tried to drag Tresh and the couch back into the living area. The current pushed at the back of his thighs, tried to bend his knees, and curled around his feet. With every step, he thought he would fall over, but he just leaned back a bit and pushed against whatever foot was flat as he lifted the other and placed it slowly behind him. There were fewer spraying holes above the waterline since it was higher, but he still tried to stay in the middle of the hall. He thought he wasn't making much progress until he saw he'd passed the kitchen and dining areas.

"Ten minutes ago I thought I was going to die. I was tripping all over and felt feeble and powerless," he muttered wonderingly, not sure whether he was talking to himself or to the unconscious Tresh. He looked down, as the water was getting higher and making it harder to place his feet. "Now I'm energetic again. Must be another adrenalin rush, or something."

"Although I'm not sure that's helping at the moment," he continued, peering at Tresh. "Hey, why are you so heavy all of a sudden?"

Michael grunted and pulled the couch, but it seemed to be stuck in place. He glanced at the other end of the couch and saw that it had swung into the doorway of the kitchen and the high end of the back was snagged on the corner of a steel shelf.

He tried pushing the couch farther in to get the shelf to let go, but the couch was stuck. He heaved up and shoved down and the couch rocked back and forth but still didn't come loose. Luckily, Tresh didn't fall off.

Finally, Michael braced a foot against the wall of the doorjamb and gave a good yank. The couch came away from the shelf with a scraping noise. He would have been thrilled, except that now the back of the couch was torn open about five inches and losing air fast.

# CHAPTER 16

Michael had to get Tresh out of the water before the couch went completely flat. The water level was almost waist-high now. It covered the top row of the holes on the wall, and the surface of the water changed to mild ripples instead of gushing waves, but underneath the current still pushed against him.

Michael began jumping forward and pulling the couch behind him with all his strength. It was like trying to run through a bowl of jelly. When he reached the area under the platform next to the ramp, he used one hand to loosen and take off his belt.

"I hate this belt," Michael said. "It's one of those webbed adjustable kinds. But if I'm right, it might just come in handy." It still seemed weird to talk to an unconscious guy, but it made him feel better to hear a voice in the hallway, even if it was his own.

Michael used his teeth to grab one end of the belt and pull out the excess to make it full length.

"Ok, Tresh. Hang tight. I'm going to try and get the buckle end through one of those gaps up on the platform."

Holding onto the couch with one hand, he tossed one end of the belt at the platform, but it wasn't high enough. He gave the toss more effort on the second try, but he threw it so hard that the belt jerked out of his hand and started to sink into the water in front of him.

Keeping one hand on the raft, he held his breath, ducked under the water, and grabbed for it. Feeling nothing, he opened his eyes underwater.

To his surprise, he could see clearly, and he easily grabbed the belt. His lungs, which should have been burning for air, seemed fine. He wondered how long he could stay down there, but he didn't have time to experiment.

He popped up, wiped the water off his face, and tossed the belt again. It dropped through the nearest gap on the grate. He pulled it through and threaded it around the rubber handle on the deflating couch, and then buckled it.

The floppy couch stayed tied in place right next to the ramp like a plump seagull hoping for handouts below a city pier.

"Now to get you off the sinking ship."

Michael dug his arms under Tresh's armpits and dragged him off the couch toward the ramp. Tresh's legs flopped into the water, and Michael lost his balance when they shifted. His own body, including his head, sank under, but he managed to hold his arms stiff above him and keep Tresh's head out of the water.

When he came up this time, Tresh's eyes were halfway open, and he looked groggily at Michael.

"What . . . what're we doing?"

Michael wanted to shout for joy, but all he said was, "We're saving you!"

Pushing and pulling, he managed to get Tresh onto the ramp above the waterline and then hoist himself up, too. As soon as he was solidly on land again, Michael found himself wishing he could get back in the water where his whole body felt lighter. His limbs felt like they were made of heavy iron as he tried to lift them.

"Can you move at all?" he asked Tresh.

"Maybe." Tresh feebly raised an arm, then bent his knee, and leaned to one side. "S-sort of."

"Can you help me get you up to the garbage pods?"

# CHAPTER 17

"Hey, bro," whispered Tresh, "I told you my name was Tresh, not Trash."

"It sounds crazy, but these pods are your best chance for getting out of here alive. They are oxygenated and pressurized. Are you able to stand up by yourself? I'm getting weaker."

Tresh frowned as he moved his legs. He was able to push himself up slightly, but he could not stand. He shook his head and lay back down on the ramp.

"Wait here."

Michael braced himself with his hands, got his legs beneath him, and scrambled up into a standing position. He swayed a bit, but then steadied and walked up the ramp to the control room. He came back with the empty oxygen he had discarded earlier, along with a screwdriver.

"Doc told me this cushioned side of the pack is made of multiple layers of folded silicone. If I can get it open and unfolded, we can use it as a sled to get you up the ramp to the pods."

Michael used the screwdriver to jab a hole in the pack, and then tore it open and unfolded the layers into a wide sheet about three feet square.

Tresh turned onto his side, allowing Michael to spread the silicone sheet under his body, and then rolled himself onto the sheet. It was just barely big enough to fit under Tresh's entire torso from head to hips. Michael grabbed the upper corners and dragged Tresh up the ramp.

He got Tresh to the nearest pod. It had a long oval hatch running up the front. Michael opened it and was thankful the pod was empty and clean. He bent over and tried to hoist Tresh up into the pod.

Drops of salt water ran down Michael's nose, a mixture of sweat and seawater dripping from his hair. He was getting tired and hot and longed to drop back into the water below. When he finally got Tresh's entire body arranged in the pod, he lifted up the makeshift sled and handed it to Tresh.

"Here. Use this as a cushion. It might help keep you comfortable."

Tresh smiled weakly. He hugged the remains of the oxygen pack to his body as if it were a life preserver, looking as scared and vulnerable as a kindergartner on the first day of swimming lessons.

"You said you'd rocket to the top. Now's your chance, WhoToober."

"Game over, bro. Finish me."

Michael closed the hatch on the pod, and then crumpled down to the metal grate. He'd been so strong, and now he was so weak. The adrenaline boost he'd had earlier must have worn off. He lay gasping for air, knowing that he still had yet to launch the pod.

He tried to focus on the instructions for the garbage pod on the wall above him. Swallowing hard, he got to his knees and started the launch sequence. Halfway through, he slid down against the wall. He wanted to close his eyes, but he had to hit the launch button. He imagined Tresh lying in the dark in the bottom of the pod, waiting helplessly, and he made one last effort to stretch up and reach the button.

Suddenly, mechanical noises rumbled behind the wall and the grate shook. The pod began to rise up, pushed by a wave of water.

# CHAPTER 18

The sun was toasting the beach at Victoria Bay, and Michael stretched his legs over the sand to absorb its heat. He leaned back, letting the rays shine on his face, trying not to disturb the patterns Tresh was carving into the sand with a stick.

"Wait, bro, that's it?"

"Well, yeah. You know the rest of the story. You made it to the top and got picked up by the trash boat, and obviously, I turned into a fish man and now I can use both forms."

"Retweet!"

"Like anyone would believe it."

"Yeah, and all that proof on my phone was ruined by the salt water, although the vids from the boat made it to the web before we got in the sub. And I got a new phone. Came in handy in the hospital, but I couldn't wait to get out of there. I'm so glad you asked me here today, bro. I got a hankerin' for info."

"So, what do you want to know?"

"Everything!"

"Can't tell you all my secrets," said Michael grinning.

Tresh laughed. "Where have I heard that before?"

Then he got serious. "I mean, it's been four months since we went down there, and I can't believe we're both alive. I got a really good feel for what your life was like when I was in the hospital. Hashtag 'breathing hell.' How did you save me and not drown while doing it?"

"Well, I didn't know it, but I was in the middle of a transition back there. I was half human and half Finn, so I needed both oxygen *and* ocean water in the right amounts. Not too much of one or the other. The system at the hotel was programmed to not only reduce the oxygen, but also to flood the house.

"When I stopped the oxygen from reducing any further, my levels were off, so I had a hard time breathing in the air. Then the program opened a valve to let water in, only it came in faster because the squid made that hole in the water inlet pipe and the water pressure pushed too much water through. That actually balanced everything back to the right proportions. It's why I felt stronger when I was half in the water."

"So, I gotta ask . . ." said Tresh, looking at Michael's neck.

"Go for it," said Michael.

"Do you have gills? 'Cause I see what look like scars under your ears on both sides of your neck, and I don't remember seeing them before."

"Yep. Remember all that strange neck pain I had before? That was my body trying to make gills. Doc doesn't know why they stick around when I'm human."

"Speaking of him, what happened to the doctor and your parents? I can't believe you got catfished by your own mom, bro."

"Everyone survived. The squid still hunts in the area, but we figured out distractions to keep it from damaging the house. We're going to live there part time and rent it to researchers when we aren't there. After all, now we know we have escape pods that humans can use in an emergency." Michael laughed and dodged the clump of seaweed Tresh tossed at him.

"Ha ha," said Tresh. "Changing subjects. So, I was wondering if you'd be interested in developing a new video game with me. I got this great idea and I want to pitch it to the makers of Alternative Existenz."

"Sounds great—what's the idea?"

"Ok," said Tresh. "So, picture this: two guys are stranded in this underwater hotel . . ."

## About the Author

Amanda Humann lives in Seattle, and likes rain, salmon, and being sleepless, but she doesn't drink coffee or chase vampires. She creates content for comics and games, but her favorite is the youth market. Recent honors for writing include the Young Adult Library Services Association's 2014 Quick Picks for Reluctant Young Adult Readers, and an Outstanding Work-In-Progress from the Society of Children's Book Writers and Illustrators Western Washington Conference in 2012.

## Questions to Think About

1. If you were in Michael's shoes and thought you were dying from an unknown lung disease, what would your last wish be? Is there someplace you'd want to go, someone you'd want to meet, or something you'd want to do? Describe your last wish and explain why you'd make it.

2. Giving a warning of what is to come in a story is called foreshadowing, and throughout *Deep Water Hotel*, there are hints about what is actually happening to Michael. Can you find the places where the story foreshadows Michael changing into one of the Finn?

3. The Finn are made-up creatures that can live under the sea. Imagine what their lives must be like. Then write a story about the Finn. Describe where they live, what they do every day, and any problems they may face while living under the sea.

## Limbo's Diner

For as long as he can remember, Hal Crabtree's family has owned Limbo's Diner. The patrons of Limbo's are unique—they are dead, waiting for their final judgment. When Hal's classmate Gwen shows up at the diner, Hal is determined to solve the mystery of her death. If he fails, the diner could close forever.

## Meltdown Town

Years in the future, the world is in the midst of an energy crisis. Best friends Liam and Grace spend their evenings sneaking around abandoned buildings. One night, they spot a man wandering in the deadly radiation zone. How can he survive? Is he an alien? A zombie? Liam and Grace have to find out.

## Sprint

Filming a sprint car race on the local track, Dylan Clarke captures racer Carlee Martin's fiery accident. The more Dylan replays the video, the more he believes that there's something suspicious about the crash. As he investigates, Dylan discovers that some of Carlee's fellow racers might have wanted to hurt her. And now, they're after him too.